THE CAST

Peter

The bird

The duck

A cat

The grandfather

The wolf

The hunters

The veterinarian

For Ann and Brenda

Atheneum Books for Young Readers • An imprint of Simon
& Schuster Children's Publishing Division • 1230 Avenue of
the Americas, New York, New York 10020 • Based upon the
original work by Sergei Prokofiev of *Peter and the Wolf* •
Copyright © 1937 (Renewed) by G. Schirmer, Inc. (ASCAP)
• International Copyright Secured. All Rights Reserved. •
Used by permission. • Illustrations copyright © 2008 by
Chris Raschka • All rights reserved, including the right of
reproduction in whole or in part in any form. • Book design
by Ann Bobco • The text for this book is set in Brothers. •
Manufactured in China • First Edition • 10 9 8 7 6 5 4 •
Library of Congress Cataloging-in-Publication Data • Raschka,
Chris. • Peter and the wolf / Serge Prokofiev ; illustrated by
Chris Raschka.—1st ed. • p. cm. • "A Richard Jackson book." •
"Based upon the original work by Sergei Prokofiev of Peter
and the wolf." • Summary: Retells the orchestral fairy tale in
which a boy ignores his grandfather's warnings and captures
a wolf with the help of a bird, a duck, and a cat. • ISBN-13:
978-0-689-85652-5 • ISBN-10: 0-689-85652-0 • [1. Fairy
tales.] I. Prokofiev, Sergey, 1891-1953. Petia i volk. II. Title. •
PZ8.R1872Pe 2008 • [E]—dc22   2008004472 1211 SCP

Each miniature stage set in this book is made of four squares of
heavy paper, cut and painted in watercolor, then glued together
to make a three-dimensional illustration.

PETER
AND THE
WOLF

retold by
chris raschka

Based upon the original work by Sergei Prokofiev of *Peter and the Wolf*

A RICHARD JACKSON BOOK   Atheneum Books for Young Readers   New York London Toronto Sydney

Here is Peter.

Here is what he says:

Look at me

Run around and climb around and skip around

In this lovely, large, lovely

Field of green.

Now watch! See me

Spin around and twirl around and jump around

In this perfect, most perfect

Place I've been.

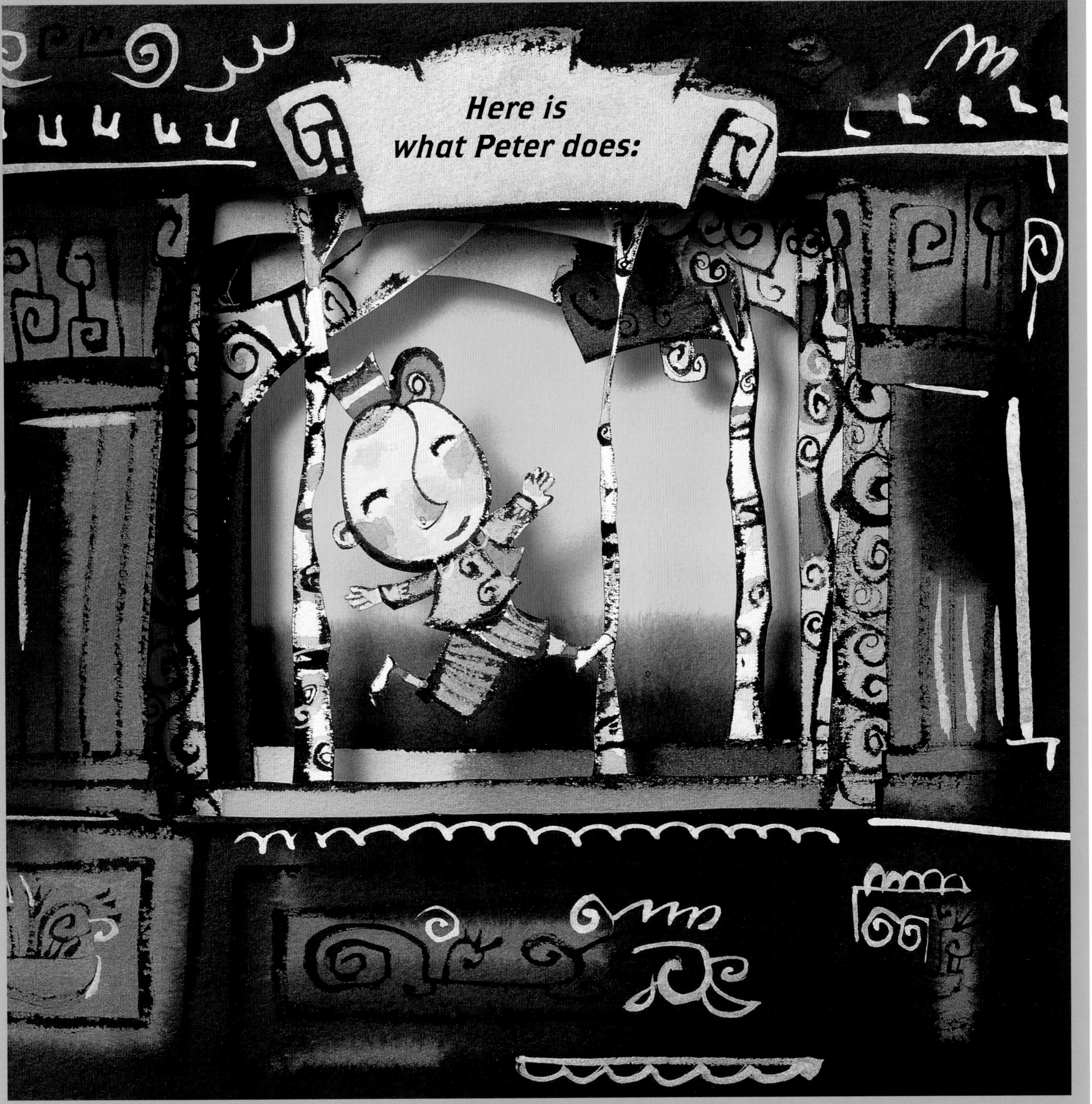
Here is
what Peter does:

Here is the bird.

Here is what the bird says:

P-Peter p-pitter P-Peter p-potter

Everythingy thingy, thingy

Izzy, izzy quiet singy.

P-Peter, P-Peter p-p-p-p-p-p

Fieldy ferny hilly dilly

Quiet, quiet stilly, stilly.

Here is the duck. *Here is what the duck says:*

Aieio,

Aieio just want tieio,

Aieio,

Aieio just want tieio

Swiiiiiiiiiiiiiiim in the

Laieaieaieaiek.

Now the bird and the duck argue.

The bird says this:

 D-ducky d-dacky d-docky d-deeky,

What kindeedle of a birdle

Ardle yoodle iffy yoodle

C-c-c-c-canty even

Fleedle floodle floadle flydle?

And the duck says this:

Waieo,

What kind of baierd

Are yoooouuuuuuuuuu if

Yaieo

Can't swiiiiiiiiiiiiiiim?

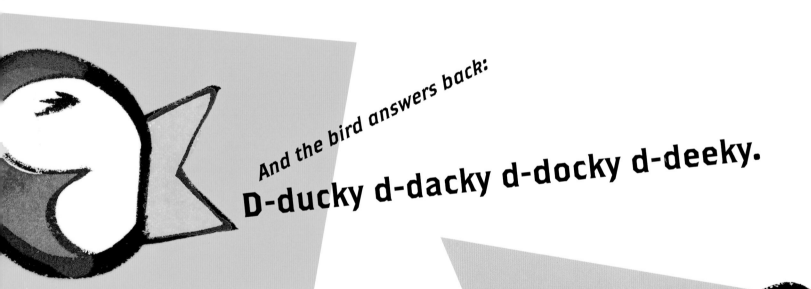

And the bird answers back:

D-ducky d-dacky d-docky d-deeky.

And the duck answers back:

Waieo, waieo, waieo, waieo.

Now a cat enters.

Here is the cat.

Here is what the cat says:

There's a bird
All alone.
There's a bird alone.
I'll just sneak up and grab him
Up and grab him now.

YUM!

But **Peter** says to the bird:

Look out!

And now they all speak at once.

The **bird** *says:*

C-catty t-tiger lion m-monster!

And the **cat** *says:*

Should I climb
Up the tree?
Should I climb the tree?
But then she'll just fly off
And leave me
Up a tree.

The **duck** *says:*

Aeio,
You're just a
Maieo, maieo, maieo
Mean old
Cahahahahahahaht.

In the middle of all this, the **grandfather** comes out.

Here is the grandfather.

Here is what the **grandfather** *says:*
I come,
I come,
To tell, to tell, to yell.
You are a
Bad, bad, bad boy,
Running away, into the field,
Out of the gate.
I come,
I come,
To say, to say,
What if a
Bad, bad, bad wolf
Came from the woods, into the field,
And you he ate?

Peter *answers this way:*

Look! I still

Run around—

I'm not afraid of wolves or you

In this perfect, most perfect

Field of green.

Nevertheless Grandfather takes Peter away.

Now here is the wolf.

Here is what he says:

BAaAaAaAH!

Gimme, gimme, gimme,
Me, meat to eat
NOW!

**Here is what the bird,
the duck, the cat, and the wolf do:**

(Oh, in the excitement, the duck foolishly jumps out of the pond.)

See what happens
between the **duck** and the **wolf**.

The **duck** says:

Aieio, aieio, aieio,

Waio, waio, waio

Aieio!

And at the same time the **wolf** says:

Gimme, gimme, gimme, gimme . . .

GULP!

(Yes, the wolf caught and swallowed her in one bite.)

Now this is how things are.

The **bird** is here.

The **cat** is there.

And the **wolf** is sometimes there,

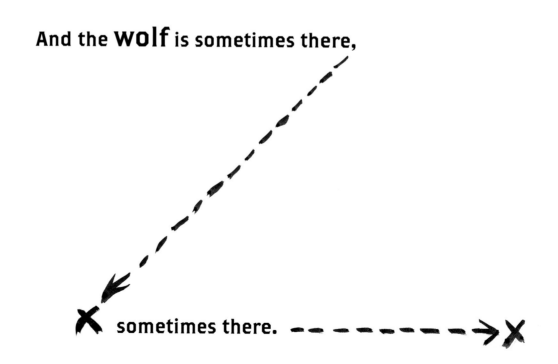

sometimes there.

And here is **Peter** again, who watches the whole thing from behind the gate.

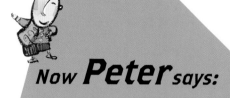

Now **Peter** *says:*

Look how I

Run around

And take this rope

And climb the wall

In this lovely, large, lovely

Field of green.

And see how I

Climb around

And grab this branch

And climb this tree

In this perfect, most perfect

Place I've been.

And **Peter** whispers something
to the bird.

Now Peter, the bird, and the wolf say this:

Peter: Watch as I swing my rope
          And twirl my rope
          And throw my rope.

The bird: P-Peter p-patter p-putter p-potter
           Needle noodle deedle doodle
           Catch me youdle doodle, doodle.

The wolf: BAaAaAaAH!

GETCHOOGETCHOOGETCHOO! . . .

And Peter: See how we trick the wolf,
We trap the wolf,
I catch the wolf
With one lucky, most perfect
Lasso toss.

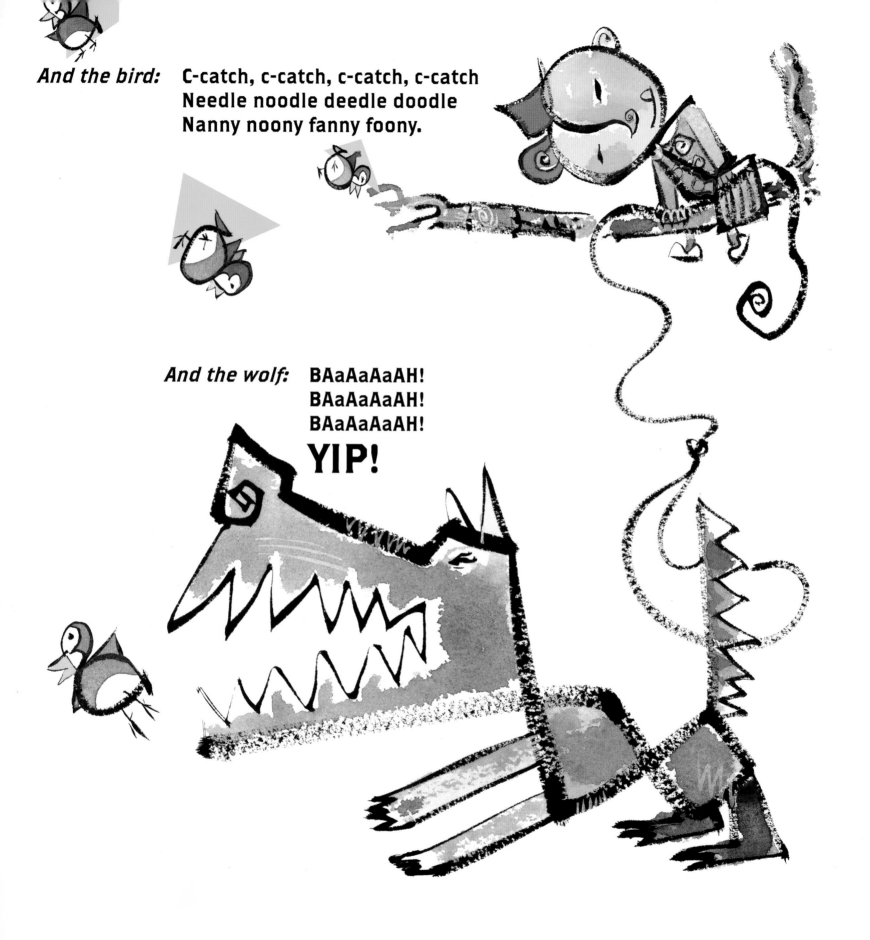

And the bird: C-catch, c-catch, c-catch, c-catch
Needle noodle deedle doodle
Nanny noony fanny foony.

And the wolf: BAaAaAaAH!
BAaAaAaAH!
BAaAaAaAH!
YIP!

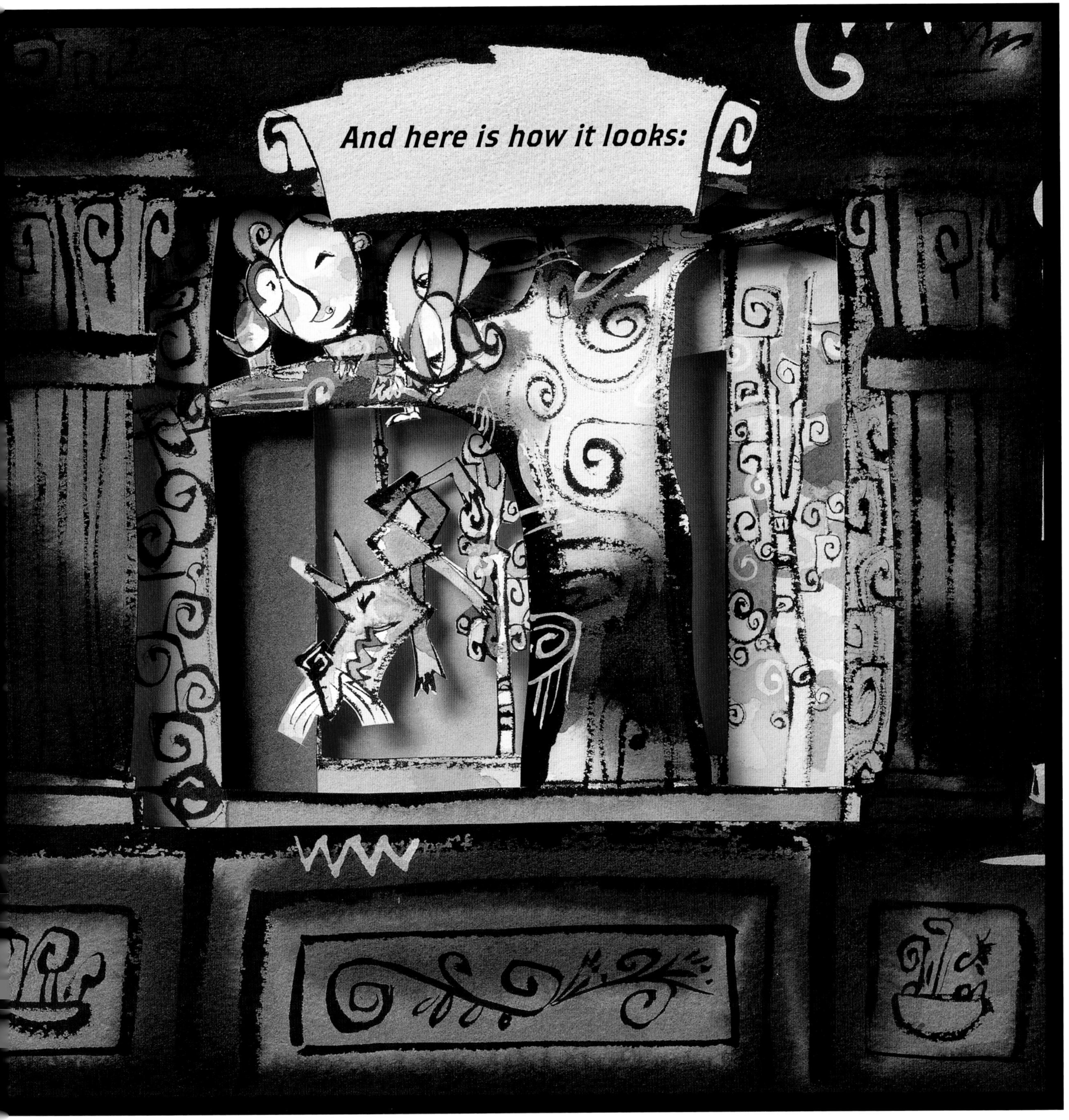
And here is how it looks:

Just then **some hunters** come out of the woods.

They shoot.
Bang, bang, bang!

Bang

BANG

Bang

BANG!

Peter says: **Don't shoot!**

Now see the triumphant procession.

Peter *shouts:*

See! Look!

Me! March!

Strong! Loud!

Fine! Proud!

The **hunters** *say:*

We are the men,

We are the men,

We are the men who hunt—

In smart fur hats,

In nice warm caps,

And fine green capes.

And we've caught the wolf!

Yes, we've caught the wolf!

See, we've caught the wolf.

He's ours.

The _wolf_ says:

WAaAaAH

GAaAaAH

Dunna, dunna like this!

RNG GRZ RLZ ZRG

BAaAaAaAH

NAH!

And the _hunters_ say:
We are the men,
We are the men,
We are the men who hunt—
In smart fur hats,
In nice warm caps,
And fine green capes.
And we've caught the wolf!
Yes, we've caught the wolf!
See, we've caught the wolf.
He's ours.

Grandfather says:
I want,
I want,
To say, to say,
And if my
Peter, Peter
Had missed the wolf?
Had thrown astray?
What would he then?

The **cat** *mutters:* **What am I**
                        Doing here
                In this hullabaloo?
                With all these lousy,
                                Noisy, silly
                                Dunderheads?
        I should leave
        And I will
                        When I know for sure
                                That nobody
                        Is giving out
        Free party bags.

And the **bird** *says:*  **P-Peter p-pitter p-patter p-putter**

L-looky, l-looky, l-looky,

Weedle deedle caught the

Wolfie, woolfie, wolfie, woolfie

Smarty, smarty, smarty, smarty.

And the **duck** quietly says:

Waio,
Waio,
Waion't someone get me
Aiou ou, ou out of here?
Waio,
Waio,
Aio wish someone would
get me
Aiaiaiaiaiaiaiaout.

And that is the story of Sergei Prokofiev's
PETER AND THE WOLF. . . .

Epilogue
The procession arrives at the zoo, where the chief veterinarian performs emergency surgery, successfully removing the duck from the wolf's stomach.